AFTER HAPPILY EVER AFTER

Goldilocks and the Just Right Club

First published in the United States in 2009
by Stone Arch Books
151 Good Counsel Drive, P.O. Box 669
Mankato, Minnesota 56002
www.stonearchbooks.com

First published by Orchard Books, a division of Hachette Children's Books.
338 Euston Road, London NW1 3BH, United Kingdom

Text copyright © Tony Bradman 2006
Illustrations copyright © Sarah Warburton 2006
The right of Tony Bradman to be identified as the author and Sarah
Warburton as the illustrator of this Work has been asserted by them in
accordance with the Copyright Designs and Patents Act 1988.

Library of Congress Cataloging-in-Publication Data
Bradman, Tony.
  Goldilocks and the Just Right Club / by Tony Bradman; illustrated by
Sarah Warburton.
  p. cm. — (After Happily Ever After)
  ISBN 978-1-4342-1304-4 (library binding)
  [1. Individuality—Fiction.] I. Warburton, Sarah, ill. II. Title.
PZ7.B7275Gn 2009
[Fic]—dc22   2008031831

Summary: After her adventure at the Three Bears' house, Goldilocks starts
a new school. She tries to fit in, but she's not a princess, a troll, or a ninja.
Goldilocks wants a group of friends who are just right for her, but that's not
so easy to find.

Creative Director: Heather Kindseth
Graphic Designer: Emily Harris

1 2 3 4 5 6 14 13 12 11 10 09

Printed in the United States of America

AFTER

HAPPILY EVER AFTER

Goldilocks and the Just Right Club

by Tony Bradman
illustrated by Sarah Warburton

STONE ARCH BOOKS
www.stonearchbooks.com

So Goldilocks apologized and everyone was ready to live happily ever after — until Mama Bear got home. **And then** ...

Capstone Press $3.99

Goldilocks felt sick as they came around the corner and she saw her house. Mom and Dad were going to be seriously unhappy.

After all, she was being marched home
by an angry grown-up. And judging by the
frown on Mrs. Bear's face as she knocked
on the front door, she was still very angry.

"Goldilocks sweetheart, where have you been?" asked Mom.

"Hi there," said Dad, noticing Mrs. Bear. "Who are you ?"

"Mrs. Bear," she said. "Your daughter broke into our cottage."

"She did WHAT?" said Dad, horrified. "Is this true, young lady?"

Goldilocks glanced up at him, nodded, and burst into tears.

Mrs. Bear told Mom and Dad the whole story. Soon they were frowning too.

Mom and Dad said they were sorry.
They couldn't understand it because
Goldilocks was a good girl, and they
would pay for the damage.

Goldilocks said she was sorry too.
Mrs. Bear seemed satisfied with that,
although she still looked pretty stern and
grumpy when she left. Goldilocks was
glad to see her go.

"I'll bet it was some kind of silly dare," Mom said. "You were with a group of friends, someone suggested it, and things got out of hand."

"No, Mom," said Goldilocks between
sniffs. "I was on my own."

Goldilocks would have loved to be part of a group of friends at school. But she'd never found the right group and didn't know why.

Earlier that day she'd felt very
unhappy about it. That's why she went
off into the woods after school instead of
coming straight home.

And the Bears' cottage had been very tempting.

She knew she'd been very naughty. But climbing trees and splashing in muddy streams had been a lot of fun.

Trying on Mrs. Bear's clothes and playing with her make-up had been cool too.

"You're not unhappy at school, are you?" asked Dad.

Goldilocks didn't answer. Mom and Dad looked at each other and raised their eyebrows.

By the end of the week, they arranged for her to transfer to a new school.

Goldilocks was surprised but pleased.
It might be a chance for her to find
some friends at last.

She felt excited when she said goodbye to her parents and walked into Forest Primary School. But she was nervous too.

"Settle down everybody," said Miss Sweet, her new teacher. The children were silent. "I'd like to introduce you to Goldilocks, your new classmate. I'm sure you'll do your best to make her feel welcome."

Goldilocks smiled shyly. Thirty pairs of eyes stared back at her, but nobody spoke. Miss Sweet made the whole class say hello.

"Don't worry, dear," she whispered to Goldilocks. "Just be yourself, and I'm sure you'll fit right in."

At recess, Goldilocks stood in the playground watching everyone.

"Hi," a smiling girl said. "I'm Little Red Riding Hood, and this is Baby Bear. We were wondering if you'd like to play with us."

"Actually, we've met before, in my bedroom," Baby Bear said. "It was all very confusing, so you probably don't remember me."

"We like to play pretending games, don't we?" said Little Red Riding Hood. "Today we're deadly Ninja warriors on a special mission."

"Thanks," said Goldilocks. "But no thanks."

Little Red Riding Hood and Baby Bear looked disappointed and walked off.

Little Red Riding Hood seemed pretty cool, thought Goldilocks. But if she made friends with Baby Bear, she might have to meet scary Mrs. Bear again.

Besides, she had decided on the group for her, the Princesses. That's what she called them, anyway.

Their names were Maisy, Daisy, Molly,
Polly, and Scarlett. They were the prettiest,
most fashionable girls in the class. They
spent every recess brushing each other's
hair and talking about clothes. Goldilocks
thought they'd be just right.

And they were for a while. But after
a couple of days she began to feel that
something was wrong. She liked being
girly, but now she realized she could get
very bored with it too.

Then one morning it poured with rain, and at lunchtime the playground was covered with puddles. Goldilocks couldn't resist jumping in them and getting wet and muddy, and soon she was having lots of fun.

But the Princesses were not impressed.

"She's not our kind of person after all. Let's go, girls," said Scarlett with her nose in the air, and the five of them turned their backs on Goldilocks.

Goldilocks was upset, but then she thought that maybe it was a good thing. So the next day she stood in the playground watching everyone again. Soon Little Red Riding Hood and Baby Bear came up to her.

"Hey, would you like to jump rope with us?" said Baby Bear.

"You must be joking," Goldilocks muttered. She still felt the same about Baby Bear, and she thought they'd stop pestering her if she wasn't nice. Besides, she had already found another group she liked.

She called them the Troll Boys. Their
names were Benny, Lenny, Harry, Barry,
and Jake. They were the loudest boys in
her class.

They spent every recess running around making as much noise as they could. Goldilocks thought they would be just right.

And they were for a while. But soon
she got the same feeling as before.
Something about this was wrong too.

She enjoyed being one of the boys.
But now she realized she could get very
bored with it as well.

Then one day the Troll Boys decided they were going to have a burping contest. They thought it was hilarious, but Goldilocks didn't.

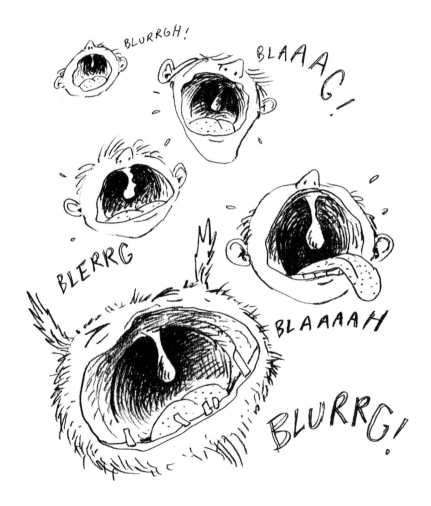

"Ugh, that's disgusting," she said.
"Count me out."

"Suit yourself," Jake said rudely. "Come
on guys, she probably wants to brush her
hair." And the five of them turned their
backs on her.

That evening Goldilocks hung out in her bedroom feeling sad. She was starting to think she would never be part of a group of friends.

"Just be yourself," Miss Sweet had said. But how could she do that? Girls didn't seem to like one side of her, and boys didn't seem to like the other.

That was why she had never fit in at her old school, and why her afternoon in the woods had been such fun.

She'd been adventurous in the woods and girly in the Bears' cottage, all in the same day. Maybe she needed some friends who liked both sides of her.

Suddenly she thought of Little Red Riding Hood and Baby Bear. Little Red Riding Hood had talked about pretending to be a deadly Ninja warrior.

Baby Bear had asked her to jump rope. They didn't seem to mind what they played as long as they had fun! They would be the perfect group for Goldilocks.

She would just have to take the risk of meeting Mrs. Bear again. So the next day at recess, Goldilocks went straight up to Little Red Riding Hood and Baby Bear and asked if she could play with them.

"Although I'd understand if you didn't want anything to do with me," she said nervously. "I mean, I know I wasn't very nice to you before."

"Really?" said Little Red Riding Hood, puzzled. "I didn't notice." Then she smiled, and so did Baby Bear, and they all went off together.

Goldilocks really enjoyed spending time with her new friends. Little Red Riding Hood liked doing girly stuff, but she had an adventurous side as well. After all, she did do karate.

And Baby Bear was a real boy, but he didn't mind playing house or holding one end of a jump rope.

And once she got to know Goldilocks better, Mrs. Bear turned out to be friendly. Although she always kept a careful eye on things.

The only problem Goldilocks had was trying to choose a name for the three of them. Then it came to her.

They weren't too girly or too rough—
they were The Just Right Club. So
Goldilocks (and Mom and Dad when they
got her report card) lived **HAPPILY EVER AFTER!**

THE END

ABOUT THE AUTHOR

Tony Bradman writes for children of all ages.
He is particularly well known for his top-selling
Dilly the Dinosaur series. His other titles include
the Happily Ever After series, The Orchard Book
of Heroes and Villains, and The Orchard Book of
Swords, Sorcerers, and Superheroes. Tony lives in
South East London.

ABOUT THE ILLUSTRATOR

Sarah Warburton is a rising star in children's
books. She is the illustrator of the Rumblewick
series, which has been very well received at an
international level. The series spans across both
picture books and fiction. She has also illustrated
nonfiction titles and the Happily Ever After series.
She lives in Bristol, England, with her young baby
and husband.

GLOSSARY

adventurous (ad-VEN-chur-us)—an exciting experience

damage (DAM-ij)—to harm something

dare (DAIR)—a challenge to do something

fashionable (FASH-uhn-uh-buhl)—a style of clothing that is popular at a certain time

muttered (MUHT-urd)—spoke in a quiet, low way

pestering (PESS-tur-ing)—annoying other people

satisfied (SAT-iss-fyed)—pleased with the end result

stern (STURN)—strict

transfer (TRANSS-fur)—to move from one person or place to another

warriors (WOR-ee-urz)—people who fight battles

DISCUSSION QUESTIONS

1. Goldilocks doesn't feel like she fits in anywhere. Describe a time when you felt left out.

2. When Goldilocks starts a new school, she feels out of place. Discuss a time that you helped someone feel accepted.

3. When Goldilocks got caught breaking into the cottage, her parents were very disappointed in her. Discuss a time that you got into trouble. What did you do to make things better?

WRITING PROMPTS

1. When Goldilocks gets caught breaking into the cottage, Mrs. Bear brings her home. Describe a good punishment for Goldilocks.

2. Goldilocks was nervous to start a new school. Write about a time that you tried something new. How did you feel?

3. Create a group you would like to be a part of. Write down the name of the group and what the group would do.

Before there was **HAPPILY EVER AFTER**,
there was **ONCE UPON A TIME** ...

Read the **ORIGINAL** fairy tales in **NEW** graphic novel retellings.

INTERNET SITES

Do you want to know more about subjects related to this book? Or are you interested in learning about other topics? Then check out FactHound, a fun, easy way to find Internet sites.

Our investigative staff has already sniffed out great sites for you!

Here's how to use FactHound:

1. Visit *www.facthound.com*

2. Select your grade level.

3. To learn more about subjects related to this book, type in the book's ISBN number: **1434213048**.

4. Click the Fetch It button.

FactHound will fetch the best Internet sites for you!